E. NESBIT
THE BOOK OF BEASTS

illustrated by
INGA MOORE

CANDLEWICK PRESS
CAMBRIDGE, MASSACHUSETTS

For Creakles,
my very own
Hippogriff

"The Book of Beasts" first appeared in *The Book of Dragons* in 1900.
For this picture book edition, the text has been abridged.

Abridgment copyright © 2001 by Inga Moore
Illustrations copyright © 2001 by Inga Moore

First U.S. edition 2001

Library of Congress Cataloging-in-Publication Data

Nesbit, E. (Edith), 1858–1924.
The book of beasts / E. Nesbit ; illustrated by Inga Moore. — 1st U.S. ed.
p.   cm.
Summary: As young King Lionel turns the pages of his magical book,
a hungry red dragon and other creatures in the illustrations come to life.
ISBN 0-7636-1579-X
[1. Fairy tales. 2. Dragons—Fiction. 3. Magic—Fiction.]
I. Moore, Inga, ill. II. Title.
PZ8.N365 Bo 2001
[Fic]—dc21   00-066685

10 9 8 7 6 5 4 3 2 1

Printed in Italy

This book was typeset in Giovanni Book.
The illustrations were done in ink, oil pastels, and oils.

Candlewick Press
2067 Massachusetts Avenue
Cambridge, Massachusetts 02140

visit us at www.candlewick.com

THE BOOK OF BEASTS

FOREWORD

THE BOOK OF BEASTS *was first published in 1900 in a collection of stories written by Edith Nesbit called* The Book of Dragons. *I was delighted to have the opportunity, one hundred years later, to bring to life once more the fearsome Red Dragon and our heroes, Lionel and the beautiful Hippogriff, which incidentally is not the Hippogriff of tradition.*

Not for a moment has it been a task. Quite the contrary, it has been fun from start to finish. For this picture book edition, I have made with great care and respect an abridgment of the text that was written, I feel sure we would all agree, by one of the finest children's writers of all time.

Inga Moore

LIONEL HAPPENED to be building a Palace when the news came. There was a knock at the door and voices talking downstairs and then, quite suddenly, Nurse came in and said:

Master Lionel, dear, they've come to fetch you to go and be King.

In the drawing room there were two very grave-looking
gentlemen in red robes with fur, and gold coronets
with velvet sticking up out of the middle
like cream in jam tarts.

They bowed low to
Lionel and said:

*Sire, your
great-great-
great-great-great-
grandfather has
died . . .*

*and now
you have got
to come and
be King.*

And they led the way to a coach
with eight white horses, which was drawn up
in front of the house where Lionel lived. It was No. 7, on
the left-hand side of the street as you go up.

So off went Lionel to be made a King. He had never expected to be a King any more than you have. All the bells of the churches were ringing like mad, and people were shouting;

Long live Lionel!

"I thought we were a Republic," said Lionel. "I'm sure there hasn't been a King for some time."

The grave gentlemen, who were the Chancellor and the Prime Minister, explained:

"Since your great-great-great-great-great-grandfather's death, your loyal people have been saving up to buy you a crown — so much a week, you know, according to people's means — sixpence a week from those who have first-rate pocket money, down to a halfpenny a week from those who haven't."

"But didn't my great-great-however-much-it-is-grandfather have a crown?"

"Yes, but he sold it to buy books. A very good King he was — but he was fond of books."

Just then the carriage stopped and Lionel was taken out to be crowned. Being crowned is more tiring than you would suppose, and by the time it was over, and Lionel had worn the Royal robes for an hour or two and had had his hand kissed by everybody, he was quite worn out, and was very glad to get into the Palace nursery.

Nurse was there and tea was ready,
and after tea Lionel said:
"I think I should like a book."
So he went down to the library,
and when Lionel came in,
the Prime Minister and the
Chancellor bowed very low,
and Lionel cried:

Oh, what
a worldful of books!
Are they yours?

"They are yours, your Majesty," answered the Chancellor. "They were the property of your great-great—"

"Well," Lionel interrupted, "I shall read them all. I love to read. I am so glad I learned to read."

"If I might advise your Majesty," said the Prime Minister. "I should *not* read these books. Your great—"

"Yes?" said Lionel quickly.

"He was a little—well, strange."

"Mad?" asked Lionel cheerfully.

"No, no,"—both gentlemen were shocked. "Not mad. The fact is, your great—"

"Go on," said Lionel.

"Was *called* a wizard."

"But he wasn't?"

"Of course not. But I wouldn't touch his books."

"Just this one," cried Lionel, laying his hands on a great brown book that lay on the table. It had gold patterns on the leather and gold clasps with turquoises and rubies in the twists. "I *must* look at this one."

For on the back in big letters he read: *The Book of Beasts*.

The Chancellor said, "Don't be a silly little King."
But Lionel had got the gold clasps undone,
and he opened the first page, and there was
a Butterfly, all red, and brown, and yellow,
and blue, so beautifully painted that it looked
as if it were alive.

"There," said Lionel, "isn't that lovely?"
But as he spoke, the Butterfly fluttered
its wings on the old yellow page
and flew up and out of the window.
"Well!" said the Prime Minister.
"That's magic, that is."

But the King had turned
the next page and there was
a shining blue bird. Under him
was written, "Blue Bird of Paradise."
The Blue Bird fluttered his wings
on the old yellow page and
spread them and flew
out of the book.

Then the Prime Minister snatched the book
away from the King and shut it, and put it on
a very high shelf. And the Chancellor said:
"You're a naughty, disobedient little King,"
and was very angry indeed.

"I don't see that I've done any harm," said Lionel.

"No harm?" said the Chancellor. "Ah, but how do you
know what might have been on the next page —
a snake or a centipede or a revolutionist,
or something like that."

"Well, I'm sorry," said Lionel. "Come,
let's kiss and be friends."

So he kissed the Prime Minister
and they settled down for a quiet
game of noughts and crosses,
while the Chancellor went to
add up his accounts.

But when Lionel was in bed he could not sleep for thinking of the book, and when the moon was shining with all her might, he crept down to the library and climbed up and got *The Book of Beasts*. He opened it, and saw the empty pages with "Butterfly" and "Blue Bird of Paradise" underneath. Then he turned the next page. There was some sort of red thing sitting under a palm tree, and under it was written "Dragon." The Dragon did not move, and the King shut the book rather quickly and went back to bed.

But the next day he wanted another look, so he got the book out into the garden, and when he undid the clasps, the book opened all by itself at the picture with "Dragon" underneath, and the sun fell full upon the page. And then, quite suddenly, a great Red Dragon came out of the book and spread vast scarlet wings and flew away across the garden to the hills, and Lionel was left with the empty page before him — empty except for the green palm tree and the yellow desert, and the little streaks of red where the paint brush had gone outside the pencil outline of the Red Dragon.

Lionel began to cry. He had not been King twenty-four hours, and already he had let loose a Dragon to worry his faithful subjects. And they had been saving up so long to buy him a crown and everything.

Then the Chancellor and the Prime Minister and the Nurse all came running to see what the matter was.

Lionel, in floods of tears, said:

It's a Red Dragon, and it's flown away to the hills.

And when the Chancellor and the Prime Minister saw the book, they said:

You naughty little King!

Put him to bed, Nurse!

And they hurried off to consult the police to see what could be done. Everyone did what they could. They sat on committees and stood on guard. They lay in wait for the Dragon but he stayed up in the hills.

Then on Saturday, in the afternoon,
the Dragon suddenly swooped down on the common
in all his hideous redness and carried off the Football
Players, umpires, goalposts, football, and all.

On the following Saturday he ate the Parliament, and an Orphanage on the Saturday after that.

Lionel was very, very unhappy. He felt that it was his duty to do something. The question was, what?

The Blue Bird that had come out of the book used to sing nicely in the Palace rose garden, and the Butterfly was very tame. So Lionel saw that *all* the creatures in *The Book of Beasts* could not be wicked, like the Dragon, and he thought:

"Suppose I could get another beast out who would fight the Dragon?"

So he took *The Book of Beasts* out into the rose garden and opened the page next to the one where the Dragon had been just a tiny bit to see what the name was. He could only see "cora," but he felt the middle of the page swelling up thick with the creature that was trying to come out, and it was only by putting the book down and sitting on it suddenly, very hard, that he managed to get it shut. Then he fastened the clasps and sent for the Chancellor, who had been ill on Saturday week, and

so had not been eaten with the rest
of the Parliament,
and he said:

What animal ends in "cora"?

The Manticora, of course.

"What is he like?" asked the King.

"He is the sworn foe of Dragons," said the Chancellor.
"He drinks their blood. He is yellow, with the body of
a lion and the face of a man. I wish we had a Manticora
here now. But the last one died years ago — worse luck!"

Then the King ran and opened the book at the page that had "cora" on it, and there was the Manticora, just as the Chancellor had described.

And in a few minutes the Manticora came sleepily out of the book, rubbing his eyes and mewing piteously.

And when Lionel said:

Go and fight the Dragon!

he put his tail between his legs and ran away. He went and hid behind the Town Hall, and at night, when the people were asleep, he went around and ate all the pussycats in the town. And then he mewed more than ever.

On Saturday morning the Dragon came looking for the Manticora, who was not at all the Dragon-fighting kind, and found him trying to hide himself in the Post Office among the ten o'clock mail. The Dragon fell on the Manticora at once, and the mewings were heard all over town. Then there was a sad silence, and presently the Dragon came walking down the Post Office steps spitting fire and smoke, and tufts of Manticora fur.

The Dragon was a nuisance for the whole of Saturday, except during the hour of noon, and then he had to rest under a tree or he would have caught fire from the heat of the sun. You see, he was very hot to begin with.

At last came a Saturday when the King said:

*Nurse, dear, kiss me in case I never come back, but I **must** try to save the people.*

"Well, if you must, you must," said Nurse, "but don't tear your clothes or get your feet wet."

So off he went.

The Blue Bird sang more sweetly than ever, and the Butterfly shone brightly, as Lionel once more carried *The Book of Beasts* out into the rose garden, and opened it — very quickly, so that he might not change his mind. The book fell open almost in the middle and there was written at the bottom of the page, "Hippogriff," and before Lionel had time to see what the picture was, there was a fluttering of wings and a stamping of hoofs, and a soft, friendly neighing; and there came out of the book a beautiful white horse with a long, long, white mane and a long, long, white tail, and he had great wings like swans' wings, and the kindest eyes in the world, and he stood there among the roses.

The Hippogriff rubbed his silky-soft, milky-white nose against the little King's shoulder. And the Blue Bird's song was very loud and sweet.

Then suddenly the King saw coming through the sky the great wicked shape of the Red Dragon. And he knew at once what he must do. He caught up *The Book of Beasts* and jumped on the back of the gentle, beautiful Hippogriff, and leaning down he whispered in the sharp white ear:

Fly, dear Hippogriff, fly your very fastest to the Pebbly Waste.

And when the Dragon saw them start,
he turned and flew after them,
with his great wings flapping
like clouds at sunset.

But the Dragon could not catch the Hippogriff.
The red wings were bigger than the white ones,
but they were not so strong, and the white-winged horse
flew away, away, and away, with the Dragon pursuing,
till he reached the very middle of the Pebbly Waste.

Now, the Pebbly Waste is like parts of the seaside — all round, loose, shifting stones, and there is no grass there and no tree within a hundred miles of it.

Lionel jumped off the white horse's back in the middle of the Pebbly Waste, and he unclasped *The Book of Beasts* and laid it open on the pebbles. He had just jumped back onto his horse when up came the Dragon.

He was flying very feebly, and looking around everywhere for a tree, for it was just on the stroke of twelve, the sun was shining like a gold guinea in the blue sky, and there was not a tree for a hundred miles.

The white-winged horse flew round and round
the Dragon as he writhed on the pebbles.
He was getting very hot: indeed, parts of him
had begun to smoke. He knew he must certainly
catch fire unless he could get under a tree. He made
a snatch with his red claws at the King and Hippogriff,
but he was too feeble to reach them, and besides,
he did not dare to over-exert himself
for fear he should get any hotter.

It was then he saw *The Book
of Beasts* lying on the pebbles,
open at the page with
"Dragon" written
at the bottom.

He looked, and he looked again, and then,
with one last squirm of rage, the Dragon
wriggled himself back into the picture,
and sat down under the palm tree,
and the page was a little singed
as he went in.

As soon as Lionel saw the Dragon had been forced to go
and sit under his own palm tree because it was the only
tree there, he jumped off his horse,
shut the book with a
BANG! and cried:

HURRAH!

And he clasped the book very tight with the turquoise
and ruby clasps.

"Oh, my dear Hippogriff," he cried, "you are the bravest,
most beautiful—"

"Hush!" whispered the Hippogriff, modestly. "Don't
you see we are not alone?"

And indeed there was quite a crowd around them on the Pebbly Waste: the Prime Minister and the Parliament and the Football Players, the Orphanage and the Manticora, indeed everyone who had been eaten by the Dragon.

You see, it was a tight fit even for a Dragon inside the book—so, of course, he had to leave them outside.

They all got home somehow, and all lived happy
ever after.

When the King asked the Manticora where he would like
to live, he begged to be allowed to go back into the book.
"I do not care for public life," he said.

Of course he knew his way back onto his own page,
so there was no danger of letting out the Dragon.
And of course he left the pussycats outside,
because there was no room
for them in the book.

As for the beautiful,
white-winged Hippogriff,
he accepted the position of
the King's Own Hippogriff.

And the Blue Bird and Butterfly
sing and flutter among the lilies
and roses of the Palace garden
to this very day.